The FAB Four

ORCHARD BOOKS
96 Leonard Street, London EC2A 4XD
Orchard Books Australia
32/45-51 Huntley Street, Alexandria, NSW 2015
ISBN 1 84121 360 8
First published in Great Britain in 2003
A paperback original
Text and illustrations © Ros Asquith 2003
The rights of Ros Asquith to be identified as the author and
the illustrator of this work have been asserted in accordance
with the Copyright, Designs and Patents Act, 1988.
A CIP catalogue record for this book is available from the British Library.
1 3 5 7 9 10 8 6 4 2
Printed in Great Britain

Three's a Crowd

a

Crowd

**Ros
Asquith**

ORCHARD BOOKS

One

"I'm not going. I'm not beginning to go. I'm not starting to begin to go. I'm not even going to *think* about going any more." Such was Owl's resolution as she stared, glummer than glum, at the yellow leaflet for *Kamp Krazy Kingdom – Where Adventure Never Ends.*

"Never ends. Huh. Never begins. Not for me. NO WAY," grumbled Owl. She scanned the brochure for signs of hope. It was packed with 'fun' activities. Hooray! White-water canoeing! Abseiling! Archery! Pole vaulting! Right up Owl's street. Not.

Yum, yum, thought Owl. I can imagine one or two things I'd rather do. Like octopus wrestling. Or perhaps sitting at the bottom of a very deep well for a week...

And the camp was on an island! Across water – virtually abroad!

I'm not even going to mention this trip to mum, Owl thought. She need never even know about it. I'll just tell the teachers that I can't go.

Relieved at this brainwave, Owl scrunched up the leaflet. Unfortunately, in Owl's bedroom, which was the size of a mouse's shoe box, or would have been, if mice had shoes, there was no waste paper bin. She glanced round, which didn't take long. Tiny bunk bed above teeny weeny desk. Postage-stamp wall covered in theatre posters. Toddler-size beanbag. Goldfish bowl. But, strong as Owl's desire to avoid her school trip was, she was not about to risk poisoning her goldfish with shredded leaflet. So, she chucked it out of the window (the leaflet, not the goldfish).

Immediately, a furious voice screeched "Litterbug!"

Typical. This was her mother's one day of the century for tidying up the garden.

"What's this? Oh. Em! Brilliant! You've got a school trip! Why didn't you tell me?"

Owl thought fast.

"N-no, it's nothing. Just something I p-picked up... at the l-library."

"Oh. Well, don't go throwing rubbish about."

Phew.

But Owl's deception lasted just three days.

On the fourth day, she returned from school to find her mother waving an official looking letter addressed to "The parent or guardian of Emily Smith..."

"Em," said her mother in her kindest voice. "The school is asking why we haven't returned the school trip forms. That Adventure Club? Remember? The one that you pretended was nothing to do with you?"

"Oh," sighed Owl.

"So, I've sent it back, with the deposit..."

"No! H-how c-could you?" cried Owl as her heart sank.

"Because everyone else will be going and it sounds lovely and I think you'll have a great time."

Owl shook her head. "No. I c-can't go. I h-hate school. I hate school t-trips. None of my friends will be there. ALL my friends are at another, n-nicer school."

Owl was thinking of her three best pals, Lizzy, Claire and 'Flash' Harriet, who, with Owl, made up the Fab Four.

"Em," said her mother kindly, "I think we need a little talk."

So, Em and her mother had a little talk. It was one of those little talks where the mother speaks a lot and the offspring gazes gloomily into the distance, wondering why they were ever born.

Mrs Smith was, naturally, trying her best to be kind. She had worried about Em since she was a small baby, and now that she was older (although still very small), Mrs Smith was still worrying.

Long ago, when little Em had held onto her legs like a limpet, whenever she tried to leave her – even at birthday parties with big chocolate cakes –

all the other mothers had said, "Oh, they're all like that to begin with. Don't you worry, she'll grow out of it." It had been the same at playgroup, nursery, primary school... But, while other shy children had grown out of it, Em never had.

Em's glamorous sister, Loretta, was a livewire, always busy, masses of friends, talented, beautiful, but Em was just... well, quieter than a mouse. Quieter than an ant, really, thought Mrs Smith – after all, mice do a bit of scuffling about and squeaking. Of course, Emily was very brainy, but her mum felt that it was time to take a stand. The shyness had to stop.

"Brains aren't everything, Em. You've got to be a bit more adventurous and get a bit of a social life. They do all these wonderful activities: white-water canoeing, abseiling...! You'll feel so silly if you're the only one who doesn't go. Loretta LOVED her school trips."

Em finally spoke. "I'm n-not Loretta. I do n-not like big groups of people. I do not like g-games and white-water canoeing. I *have* got a social life. I've got the Fab Four. And if you'd sent me to the same school as them, I might have been a happy p-person!"

And with that, she stomped upstairs and wept into the goldfish bowl. (Which wasn't a very good idea, as she then had to spend half an hour cleaning it out in the sudden fear that salt water might change the goldfish into a shark).

Mrs Smith sighed.

When he got home, Mr Smith sighed.

When she got home, big sister Loretta sighed.

"It's all my fault," said Mrs Smith. "I should have made her go out and about more when she was little – I mean, younger."

"Oh, shush," said sensible Mr Smith sensibly. "She'll come out of her shell in her own good time."

"Look, I'll ring Claire. She'll cheer Em up," volunteered Loretta.

Sure enough, bouncy, kind Claire (Eclaire to her closest mates) came bouncing straight round and lolloped upstairs to bang on Em's door.

But Em wouldn't open up.

"Owl. Owly!" cooed Eclaire.

"Go away. I'm d-drowning myself."

"What? In the goldfish bowl?"

"Yes. I'm small enough."

"I've got some Nuclear Nougat." Nuclear Nougat was Em's favourite out of the many amazing sweets Eclaire made.

"I know I'm small, but I'm not f-five years old," sighed Em. "You think Nuclear Nougat can compensate me for the agonies of my soul?"

"Oh, Owl, don't be daft. It's only a stupid school trip."

"They t-told you? You mean you came round here just because you knew that I d-didn't want to go on the school trip?" And Em burst into more tears.

Standing on the other side of the door, Eclaire felt worried. Owl was shy, sure, but not a cry baby. She decided tough talk might work.

"I've called a meeting of the Fab Four!" Eclaire yelled. "My place, tomorrow, at six. Be there or be a wimp. Byeeeee."

Owl felt thoroughly ashamed of herself. She hadn't opened her door to dear old bouncy Eclaire. She had shouted at her dear old worried mum. And she might have poisoned dear old Goldy, who was, after all, a freshwater fish. She *was* a wimp. She spent the next half hour changing the furniture in the goldfish bowl. Goldy could now choose from a cheerful skull, a decorative, ruined castle and a pirate's cannon. She wondered, from time to time, whether he really cared about these things, but she felt he should have some variety.

Then she spent ten minutes blowing her nose and making resolutions. Of course, she decided that she would go to the school trip. It wasn't walking through flames, after all. In fact, it felt much worse than that to Owl. But she told herself that it would be OK and bounced down to tea with a wide smile.

"Sorry about that," she grimaced. "Of c-course I'll go. I'm sure I'll just *love* it to pieces, just I-like

Loretta." She threw her big sister what she hoped was a withering look.

"Are you all right Em? You look very cheerful. You're not running a fever are you?" asked her mum.

"Some people are never satisfied," huffed Mr Smith.

Owl kept up her pretence at breakfast next morning and went into school with a smile so broad it hurt her jaw. Several people asked if she was all right.

"Just fine," she retorted, in an unusually loud voice (almost as loud as a butterfly sneezing), and breezed into class. Everyone was crowded round a noticeboard headlined *Kamp Krazy Kingdom – Where Adventure Never Ends.*

Pinned on it were brochures and lists. Owl's heart skipped a beat. The lists were of cabins they had been allocated. Four in some, six in others.

"Please, please let me be in a cabin with Mrs Ironglove and no one else," whispered Owl to herself.

Mrs Ironglove was the drama teacher who, despite having a voice like a crocodile with laryngitis and the mannerisms of a gorgon, was the only person in the school that Owl felt understood her.

"Oh, please let it be Ironglove." Owl clenched her teeth and approached the noticeboard.

But the first words she heard were: "Oh, baloney, look who we've ended up with."

"Ugh. Emily *Smith*!"

"Shhhhhh! Look who's here!" Three girls called Bernice, Sylvie and Mathadi, kicked each other and turned round to peer at Owl, who walked calmly by, biting her lip, pretending she hadn't heard a word.

Bernice and Sylvie giggled, but Mathadi came up to Owl later and said, "Sorry about that. They didn't mean nothing by it."

"I don't know what you're talking about," mumbled Owl, blushing.

"Suit yourself," said Mathadi, running off.

Great, thought Owl. Someone tried to be nice to me – and I blew it. I've ended up with big bully, bossy-boots Bernice, smirking, soppy, stupid Sylvie and meek, mild, mealy-mouthed Mathadi, who won't want to speak to me ever again. I have got the worst, the very, very worst group of girls I could possibly have had in the whole world, I have to find a way to escape.

Two

"All for one and one for all
Fatty, skinny, short and tall
Frizzy, Flash, Owl and Eclaire
Stick together, foul or fair."

"I declare this Emergency meeting of the Fab Four open," said Eclaire, who was reclining luxuriously in a nest of enormous teddies.

Eclaire's bedroom was exactly like her: spacious, cosy and warm. Soft toys and enormous beanbags filled every space, the bed was covered in a mass of satin, patchwork and velvet cushions, and the walls were decorated with posters of mouth-watering food.

Owl's favourite poster was of an ice cream topped with

banana, Smarties, cherries and Liquorice Allsorts. Looking at it made her strangely happy. She realized that she hadn't felt happy for a week. Thank heaven for the Fab Four.

"Right, Owly. You don't want to go on your school trip," said Flash. "But we've all got to go on ours. Ours is the same week as yours, so we wouldn't see anything of you anyway. You'd be stuck at home all alone."

Flash was her usual, spirited, practical self. Of course she would love a school trip. She was sporty, funny and up for anything. "See, it looks great!" she said, comparing the brochures. "It's got most of the same stuff as our trip. I can't wait to do the water polo!"

Owl, Lizzy and Eclaire threw each other quick looks and Eclaire was forced to stifle her giggles in a fit of sneezing. None of them wanted to disillusion the pony-mad Flash, but they all knew that water polo was just standing about in a pool throwing each other a ball. Obviously, Flash was sure that there would be horses involved somehow.

"Did I say something?" Flash asked, irritated.

"It's just that what you like and what Owly likes are not necessarily the same thing," said Lizzy, coming to the rescue. "Also, not meaning to be rude or anything, but Owly is a bit shy, and, um, not exactly sporty and these activities are all quite physical, aren't they?"

"You're telling me," said Eclaire. "I'm dreading it too, you know. Can you imagine *me* abseiling? I doubt if they'll have a rope strong enough. I'll look like a boulder on elastic. And how on Earth will I fit into a white-water canoe?"

"But there's cookery," said Lizzy. "You'll be able to bunk off and make sweeties all day, I bet. *And* you'll be with us. Oh, sorry Owl."

Lizzy glanced round to see a tear at the corner of Owl's eye. She was desperately trying to blink it back, but, so far, this meeting, which had been supposed to cheer her up, was having exactly the opposite effect. All the others had each other. She would be alone. And not just alone, but with the trio from hell: Sylvie, Bernice and Mathadi.

"But think, Owly. You'll be able to get away from Loretta for a whole week," Lizzy burbled on. "I

can't wait to get away from Ernie and his Doom Warriors. And I'll be able to make a mess! Heh, heh! Without Mum nagging me to tidy up all the time."

"B-but I *like* my family," whispered Owl. "I've never been away from home before."

This was greeted with stunned silence.

"What, never?" gasped Flash. She adored her mum, but was always keen to get out of their tiny flat at every opportunity, especially when, like this, the school was paying for the free-school-dinner-pupils like her that couldn't afford the trip.

"You've stayed the night with us," said Flash.

"That's true," said Owl. "But I've only ever been on Fab Four sleepovers. I've n-never stayed with anyone else."

"Not even an auntie or someone like that?" asked Flash, more and more surprised.

"No, *and* I've never been abroad before," Owl added. "I've only ever b-been to Littlehampton."

"But the island where the camp is isn't abroad," bellowed Flash. "It's only a little ferry ride away." Her voice trailed off as she looked at Owl's face.

"Oooooh, poor Owly. Let's look more closely at your brochure. I bet there'll be drama," said Eclaire encouragingly, anxious to change the subject. She hadn't been away much on her own either, and she secretly wondered whether, if she hadn't been going with the rest of the Fab Four herself, she might feel just like Owl.

The four girls scanned the brochure. But no. No drama. Not even a tiny bit of dance. No art either.

"Typical. You spend all day at school for months doing horrible SATS, endless maths and science—"

"Don't knock science," interrupted Lizzy, who intended to become an inventor.

"...and hardly any art or drama or music," continued Eclaire, "and then off you go on a school trip and you're suddenly supposed to get all active and be an Olympic pentathlon winner, with *no* practice, and you can't even refuse to join in. It's all very organized, isn't it?" Eclaire was beginning to think maybe she wouldn't go either. Suddenly, she had a brainwave.

"I know, Owly. We'll swap. I'll stay at home cooking you all a big feast for your return and you can go as me!"

The other three gazed at Eclaire as though she needed a brain transplant.

Eclaire giggled and shrugged. "It's obvious that I'm dreading this trip as much as Owl is," she admitted. "I think the only solution is a nip of Nuclear Nougat and a few buns."

Eclaire rolled off to top up the Fab Four's feast.

Meetings at her house were always the most popular, because she always made amazing food, whereas everyone else just got a few biscuits and crisps together at the last minute. But there was a gloomy atmosphere, all the same.

Lizzy realised how much they always relied on Eclaire to be calm and cheerful. The only thing that ever seemed to upset her was when her mother, the amazingly thin Mrs Pinn, was nagging her to diet. But now even Eclaire was being distinctly wobbly and failing in her duty to cheer up Owl.

Lizzy decided to do the job for her. "Listen, Owl. See this as a challenge. Why don't you use it to improve your acting skills? You know drama is what you're brilliant at — apart from thinking, of course, you're better at thinking than all the rest of us put together — but let's concentrate on the acting for now. Go on the trip. And *act* like you're enjoying it. Then maybe you'll find you really *are* enjoying it after all."

"Yeah," said Flash. "That's a brilliant idea. I'm sure that will work."

But Owl could see Flash was doubtful. Flash never acted. With her, what you saw was what you got. Well, thought Owl, I suppose I *could* give it a try...

At this point, Eclaire surged back in with a whole plate full of Nuclear Nougat just for Owl and an iced bun each. Owl was touched.

"Sorry, Owly. I know this meeting was supposed to be about you and it's ended up being as much about me," said Eclaire ruefully. "It's made me realise that I really don't want to go *at all*. But I've got to, because my mum's paid and I'll feel a complete dork if I don't." Then she added, "But I know it's worse for you, because I've got Lizzy and Flash and you haven't. So we'll just have to text message each other, or something."

"You're not allowed to take m-mobile phones," said Owl glumly.

"There are ways," said Eclaire, mysteriously. "Anyway, we'll all send you a postcard every day. Then, everyone will realise what a popular person you are, if you get three cards a day."

"Or six," added Flash. "We could write you two each."

Owl felt even more lonely when they said that. She had good friends, sure, but they were all in this

25

room. There was no one that she felt at all comfortable with in her school. No one at all.

"So, you'll go. You'll act all the time. You'll pretend to enjoy it. You won't write tragic letters home. You won't ring up begging to come back. And it'll be over in a flash. Is that agreed?" said Lizzy, being alarmingly business-like and marking off all these points on her fingers.

"Yeah, OK," said Owl, acting happy.

Great," said Eclaire, relieved that Owl looked so much more cheery. "I now declare this meeting of the Fab Four closed."

The girls chanted:

"Four for one and one for four
Funny, clever, rich and poor
Frizzy, Flash, Eclaire and Owl
Stick together, fair or foul."

And then they all shouted, "Meringue!" and the meeting was over.

Owl went home looking very cheerful. But she knew in her heart that she couldn't face it. Finally, she decided, as she said goodnight to Goldy, who made no response and continued to swim about forlornly, that she would do exactly as the Fab  Four suggested. She would do everything she had promised. Not write letters home, not phone up begging to be brought home and she would act *all* the time. But with one major difference. She would act ill. Then she wouldn't have to write home, because she would be *at* home. In bed.

Heh, heh, heh, thought Owl — and drifted into the first untroubled sleep she had enjoyed for days.

Three

Owl spent the next few days being artificially bright and bubbly. Her mother smelt a rat, but decided to say nothing. Her worst fears were confirmed when, two days before the school trip, Owl complained of a bad stomach ache.

"Just something you ate," said her mum.

"And my throat feels as if a herd of d-dragons is practicing fire-breathing in it."

"Just something you said," said her mum.

"And *both* my ears feel as though a small army of b-builders is drilling from the inside."

"Just something you heard," said her mum.

"I'm sure I've got a f-fever," continued Owl.

"I'm sure you haven't. You'll be late for school."

"Oh, it would be *awful* to miss the school trip. I do hope I'm not coming down with that bug that killed all those people in N-Norfolk" said Owl finally.

"What bug?" asked her mum, who was now becoming alarmed.

"Oh, nothing. I'm sure I'll be f-fine" smiled Owl bravely, picking up her rucksack with a stifled groan and hobbling off, leaving her poor mother feeling guilty.

Sure enough, the phone at Mrs Smith's office rang at lunchtime. And an anxious-sounding woman asked her if she could come over to the school to pick up Owl. "She's very poorly," said Mrs Clamp, the easily fooled school nurse.

"Hmmm," said Mrs Smith.

However, when she got there, Owl's mum found that her daughter did indeed look very poorly, and she began to wonder if Owl was really ill after all.

Owl acted her heart out. She had sniffed quite a lot of pepper, so she was sneezing convincingly, but wished she hadn't, because her nose felt extremely hot and itchy. She had wiped her forehead with a damp tissue to make it look convincingly beaded with sweat, and she had kept her eyes open for several minutes without blinking, which made them red and sore. The next bit was easy – gently warm the thermometer to give a convincing temperature of, say, 101 degrees. She didn't want her mother panicking and calling a doctor yet.

But her mum did panic a bit. She asked Owl to look at a bright light and put her chin on her chest. She checked all over her for any weird spots. Then she tucked her up in bed with a copy of *The Beano*.

"Sorry, love. I thought you were putting it on this morning," she said.

Owl felt bad about that. But not bad enough to own up. She only had to keep this up for a couple of days and then she would be home free.

"Doctor tomorrow, if you're not better."

Owl snuggled down to read her Shakespeare. Of course, she loved *The Beano*, but she had to admit that she was growing out of it and only read it when she was ill. She was touched that her mother had got it for her, but she couldn't read Shakespeare at school – everyone would take the mickey.

At school she read the same books as everyone else. The big craze was for *Spine Thrillers*, a ghost series. Owl had read the most recent one, which was about an evil ghost doctor who entered the

the nice local GP and poisoned his patients.
...dmit, it had put her off doctors...

...this is nice, thought Owl, snuggling
...pile of Eclaire's Chocwhizzers and Hamlet.
...yum.

But the very next day, Owl was bored.

"Only one day and I'm fed up already," she thought. Her mother had, very unkindly in Owl's opinion, gone off to work in the morning, although she did come home at lunchtime. Owl took the opportunity put on her best acting display yet, forcing her poor mum to take the afternoon off work.

Owl pretended to snooze for most of the afternoon, occasionally calling for weak orange juice and moaning gently.

But, her mum was looking increasingly worried and Owl was feeling increasingly guilty.

At four thirty, the phone rang.

Mrs Smith took the call and then came and stood in Owl's doorway.

"Amazing news, Em. That was Eclaire. She, Harriet and Lizzy are going to *Kamp Krazy Kingdom* too. There was some sort of mix-up with their school's booking, so they've been re-routed. What a pity," she added, peering steadily at her daughter. "You probably won't be well enough to go, so you'll miss being there all together... Now, I'll just do a bit of shopping and then phone the doctor again."

Owl sat up, looking remarkably well. Remembering, she sank back on her pillow and groaned.

But while her mum nipped off to the shops, Owl phoned Eclaire. "What's this about you going to *Kamp Krazy Kingdom*?" she shouted in her loudest voice, which was still barely above a whisper.

"Yeah. It's true!" squealed Eclaire. "And there are only three schools going, so I bet we'll be able to meet up. Maybe we can even wangle you a place in our cabin!"

"Hey, that would be f-fabtastic," said Owl.

"Hang on, Owly. Your mum said you were out cold with bubonic plague."

"Oh. Um. Yes. I think it's, er, lifting," mumbled Owl.

"Naughty thing. Dooooooo come."

"I just m-might," said Owl.

She climbed back into bed. Only two days of pretending to be ill and she was already climbing the walls with boredom. She might as well get better and go.

When Mrs Smith returned with a large box of tissues and some Hot Lemon Gob Soothers and, touchingly, a copy of the new *Beano*, she found her daughter sitting up in bed, saying that she felt remarkably better. She even felt well enough to totter downstairs and take a turn around the garden.

Later that evening, Mrs Smith said to Mr Smith, "She was putting it all on, I'm quite sure. She cheered up immediately her friend rang."

"Don't mention it," said wise Mr Smith.

So Em's mum buttoned her lip and made Loretta do the same.

Sure enough, Owl came downstairs ready for school the next morning, still trying to look a bit ill for form's sake and declaring she felt she 'ought' to go on the trip.

"Hey, you know that bug you thought you had? said Loretta. It often seems to clear up for a day. But then it turns into leprosy within three days and all your limbs drop off. So, if you don't like the school trip, just ring up and we'll come and give you the antidote, and then we'll bring little diddums home."

"Oh, shut up, L-Loretta," Owl replied, flicking a Krunchy Pop at her.

But she was relieved not be telling lies any more. Relieved to be going after all. Forcing herself to think positively. Now, she would have to act as though it was fun...

The Fab Four got together at Owl's that evening for a planning meeting. They all squashed into Owl's miniscule room to examine the layout of *Kamp Krazy Kingdom — Where Adventure Never Ends.*

Owl's hut looked as though it was only about 500 metres from the rest of the Fab Four. And, best of all, there was only one big dining hall. Fantastic. Even in different groups, they'd be able to meet up every day, maybe even as much as three times a day!

"Mind you, I'm feeling a bit ropy myself," said Eclaire.

"Oh, come on. If Owly can do it, you can too," shouted Flash and Lizzy.

"No, actually, I really d-don't think so," said Eclaire, looking distinctly queasy.

The others stared at her in amazement.

"What is it, Eclairykins?" whispered Owl, attempting to put her tiny arm round Eclaire. This reminded the others of a baby sparrow trying to put its wing round a bison.

"We saw the video of last year's trip," mumbled Eclaire.

"Yeah, it was great," said Flash.

"Hilarious," added Lizzy.

"Hmm. Sure," muttered Eclaire. "I suppose you noticed that... big boy?"

"What, Fatty Ferdy?" laughed Flash. "Yeah, wasn't he a hoot?"

"He couldn't do any of the sports," honked Lizzy. "Remember when he fell into the river and splashed old Ratfink Weasel Eyes? It was like a tidal wave! From just one boy! I thought I'd die laughing."

"Well, I didn't," said Eclaire coldly.

"Who's Ratfink Weasel Eyes?" asked Owl in the chilly silence that followed, trying vainly to stretch her arm further round Eclaire.

But no one was listening.

"Look, Eclaire, that was stupid. It's not because Ferdy's f...big. I mean, everyone likes him."

"And we never *think* of you like that."

But they'd *said* it.

It was Owl who came to the rescue. "Eclaire. I know exactly h-how you feel. You're too big. I'm too small. I won't be able to reach the ropes on all those horrible assault courses. I bet everyone will laugh at that. If you f-fall in the river and make a tidal wave, everyone will laugh at you, too. You'll just have to t-try not to fall in the river. Or if you do, enjoy making everyone laugh. Or pretend you've started your period so you can't go on the h-horrible bits. There are *always* some kids who don't do all the horrible bits. And they can be you and me! We'll sit in the dining-room together making up p-poems and p-plays and... and... m-menus. I promise that anything you don't go on, I won't go on either."

Eclaire sat quietly, looking at her feet, then she asked Owl for a bit of paper.

Everyone had to get up and squash onto the tiny bunk to make room for Owl to open her desk drawer.

Eclaire took the bit of paper and a felt tip and scribbled for ten minutes. The other three watched anxiously. Was it a confession? A goodbye-I'm-leaving-the-Fab-Four-for-ever note?

Then Eclaire handed Owl this:

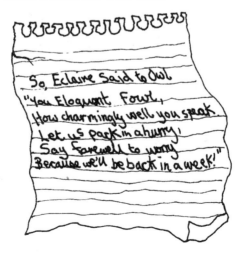

So, Eclaire said to Owl
"You Eloquent Fowl,
How charmingly well you speak.
Let us park in a hurry,
Say farewell to worry
Because we'll be back in a week!"

"Eclaire. You are truly amazing. You'll be the first poetic chef. Who cares if you can't abseil? You will open the first poetry cafe with rhyming menus," said Lizzy.

" You can call it BUNS R FUN," laughed Flash.

And, for the moment at least, all of the Fab Four felt relieved and happy. They were mates, after all, and five days in *Kamp Krazy Kingdom* was bound to have something positive to offer, wasn't it?

Four

That night, 180 children, 60 from each participating school, packed their bags for the school trips to *Kamp Krazy Kingdom.*

Of those children 160 had a worry. Each one of them thought they were the only one with a worry. Here are some of their worries:

There were much worse worries than these ones, too. But the next day dawned, and every child went off, except one who had hysterics when she saw the coach and had to be taken home and then spent the whole week wishing she had gone.

Owl had bounced out of bed, absolutely determined to enjoy herself. She had also decided to pretend that she wasn't, in her letters home. She thought her parents and Loretta deserved a little bit of pain. They had *not* been sympathetic — well apart from her mum — and it would be *fun* to wind them up a bit.

As well as Mrs Ironglove, the teachers were accompanying Owls' school. Mrs Spindle was the tall thin music teacher who spoke in a voice so high that only bats and extremely quiet children could hear her. Miss Rotunda was the completely spherical Italian maths co-ordinator who was terribly jolly and always liked to start her class with this jovial remark:

"Once you've seen me, you've seen a sphere.

Nothing to fear from saying sphere.

A circle is flat and a sphere is fat, so be of good cheer."

And then she would grin from ear to ear, looking disconcertingly like the Cheshire Cat from

Alice in Wonderland.

And, last but by no means least, there was the horrifying figure of Mr Vim, the grisly PE teacher.

Mr Vim was like something out of a book on Victorian schools. When he whispered, gales blew and it was rumoured that his shouts had deafened several generations of pupils. There were plenty of children at Owl's school who would rather be put in a forest full of starving wolves than throw a ball about with Mr Vim. Hiding under desks and running to the loo to avoid him was the best exercise most of his pupils got. But, thank goodness, Owl was in Ironglove's 'care group', along with the kind, if eccentric, Mrs Spindle. The gods were smiling on Owly after all.

To Owl's horror, as the bus was starting up, she saw her mum and Loretta running towards it with the biggest teddy in her collection.

"No! I don't n-need him! Take him away!"

"But you always have him in bed," said her mum loudly.

"Not this w-week!" hissed Owly. "I've got Bunny," she whispered.

"Oh, you've got Bunny!" shouted Loretta. "That's OK, then."

Owl's cheeks burned. She was sure that everyone was laughing at her. But of course, they weren't. The poor boys had all left their cuddly toys behind, for fear of being laughed at, but most of the girls had one hidden in their luggage.

As the bus lurched off, Owl's stomach lurched too. This was it then.

The figures of Loretta and her mum diminished. It would be five whole days and four whole nights before she saw them again. But at least the rest of the Fab Four would be setting off about now too. She would see them this evening. Owl got a window seat, disguised her book with a copy of *The Beano* and settled down for a good read.

"Is this seat taken?" said a small voice.

Owl peered up to see tiny Brian Hayseed, the boy in her year who had once played a tree stump in the school play. Brian was the only child her age in the school who was smaller and almost as shy as her. She breathed a sigh of relief.

"What group are you in?" he asked.

"Ironglove's," smiled Owl smugly.

"I'm in Vim's," mumbled Brian.

"Oh. Poooooor you," said Owl, determined to cheer him up with some of Eclaire's Munchettes. There was nothing like finding someone in a worse situation than you, thought Owl, to make you feel better about things. The boys were even worse bullies than the girls if you were small and weedy, she thought.

And the idea of poor little Brian being at the mercy of Mr Vim for five days was more than she could bear.

"Maybe you could s-swap?"

"I tried," he grimaced, biting his lip.

Brian and Owl spent the whole trip playing noughts and crosses and swapping sweets. He had an amazing supply of truly disgusting varieties like spinach and mushroom gum drops, but Owly was so happy to have a friend that she gave him nearly half her emergency midnight-feast ration of Munchettes. He stuffed them into his bag and emitted a pathetic squeak. Owl glanced over to see Brian blushing deeply. He tried to hide the evidence, but Owl had already spotted a little blue fluffy rabbit peeping out of the top of his rucksack.

"Oh, don't worry," whispered Owl. "I've got my b-bunny with me too."

"Yeah, but none of the boys will have," muttered Brian. "I'm gonna have to lose him."

"I'll look after him," offered Owl. "They'll get on just fine."

Blushing like a street light, Brian sneaked his battered old blue bunny over to Owl, who introduced him to her pink and yellow one.

"Hello, what's your name?" she squeaked.

"Er, Bunny. What's yours?" she squeaked in a slightly higher pitch.

"Bunny."

"Are you looking forward to the trip?"

"No. I'd rather be home in my cosy bed with Brian."

"So would I. I mean, with Owly."

"Owly?" interrupted Brain, amazed. "Who's Owly?"

"Shh!" said Owl. "It's, um, just a n-nickname. No one at school knows it. Tell anyone and you're d-dead!"

Brain recoiled. "I won't, don't worry. But will you promise to pretend my bunny is yours?"

"Promise on the earth,
Promise on the sky
Promise on the sun
Or poke me in the eye."

Owl stuffed both the rabbits into her bag. She felt extremely happy. She had a friend.

When they arrived at the camp, Owl got quite excited, despite herself. There were three separate encampments, each with two adult camp leaders. The cabins were all made like little wooden huts in a Wild-West film. Each school had a group name. Owl's schoolmates were Apaches. The other teams were Mohican (which the rest of the Fab Four were in) and Comanche. Owl's camp was a whole 500 metres away from the Fab Four's camp, but they were all going to be together for supper. At least that would be fun. But as soon as she started to think this, Owl's heart sank again. Her camp leaders, Hawkeye and White Dove, were announcing that all the teams would be given points for activities! And the winning team would get a trophy! Argh! Now she not only had to take part in everything, but she would have to do it well!

"I wonder if we could get you into another team," said Bernice nastily. "And that little wimp with you."

Brian blushed like a pillar box.

"But first," shouted Hawkeye, who was resplendent in a chieftain's hat. "Chow."

"That means food," added White Dove.

Everyone crowded round to look at the menu. Help! It was things like "Coyote Casserole" and "Skunk Stew".

KAMP KRAZY KINGDOM
"where ADVENTURE never ends"

MENU

Coyote Casserole
Skunk Stew
Racoon Ratatouille
Bison Burger
Yahoo Pie
Fries
<u>Vegetarian option:</u>
Eggs Sunnyside down

But, of course, the food turned out to be variations of bangers and mash and pizza.

After supper, they did archery. Owl broke three arrows and lost one. Some of the boys in Comanches were fooling about and Owl got jabbed by the end of the bow. However, it looked worse than it was, and the boys team had eight points taken off their score. Unfortunately, they retaliated by tripping Owl up later, when no one was watching, and sending her brand new rucksack flying into the white-water river, soaking the two rabbits.

"Oops," sneered one of the Comanches. Didn't think you'd have anything important in it. Rucksacks are only meant for notebooks and packed lunches."

Owl was determined to get back at them by scoring ten out of ten bullseyes. Unfortunately, not only did she not score a single bullseye, she actually did not hit the target at all. This was quite pathetic really, as it was a very big target and even Brian Hayseed had hit it three times.

But Bernice scored six bullseyes, so Apaches won.

"No thanks to you-know-who," snorted Bernice that night. "And if you keep getting points by cheating, the Mohicans'll probably raid our cabin in the night and *scalp* us!"

"I d-didn't cheat. He hit me with his b-bow," said Owl, who was thoroughly ashamed.

"Huh. This place is a dump. Did you read the menu? Pathetic Wild-West-style jokes. I suppose *you're* a veggie and you'll be eating those disgusting soy-bean burgers," Bernice said scornfully to Owl.

Owl couldn't be bothered to deny it. Anyway, she had been thinking of being vegetarian after seeing a film about battery chickens. She just sat quietly while she watched Bernice bagging the best bunk, using all the coathangers (only four) in the tiny cupboard and even trying to take an extra blanket off Mathadi's bunk. She's such a bossy boots, Owl thought. But she decided that this was not the time to get into a fight.

"Night, all," she whispered and tumbled into dreamland.

Five

After breakfast, there was half an hour of free time. Owl met up with the rest of the Fab Four who were all whingeing about the weedy Petula, who was sharing their cabin.

"Talk about a cry baby," snarled Flash. "She just moans and moans on about how she would like to be with her mates. I don't know why they've put her in with us. She says she hates everyone in our school, anyway, and all her friends are at some other school."

"Yeah, some people just don't know how to make the best of a bad job," added Lizzy.

"Like m-me," said Owl quietly.

"Whoops," said Eclaire, throwing Lizzy a fierce look. "Look, let's cheer ourselves up by writing home," she said. So they did.

Owl's letter:

Dear Mum and Dad and Loretta,

It is fine here, although the food seems to be mainly fried weasel, or maybe ferret. The cook said that it's fried in diesel oil, although it tastes a bit worse, so maybe it's petrol. I think the mattresses have pebbles in and some thorns also, but I am fine although of course I didn't sleep a wink.

The weather is fine except for the rain, which is falling all the time. It's that big fat kind of rain where every drop is like a bucket of water tipped on your head. Never mind, Mr Vim says it's good to get fresh air, even though a couple of kids were struck by lightning last year with, I believe, fatal consequences.

We did archery the minute we arrived, and some of the boys were a bit silly with the equipment, but I didn't get too badly injured and the doctor said he's sure my sight will be fine. We are doing abseiling tomorrow and Mr Vim says they haven't got the proper safety helmets, but never mind. I'm sure I'll be fine. If you want to come and get me, that would be OK. Otherwise, I'll see you soon - if I survive. Please remember to feed Goldy. It would be sad if we both died.

Love,
Emily

P.S. By the way, you know that new rucksack you bought me especially for the trip? It was trampled by a cow! And then snatched by a passing dog and hurled in the river and swept away for ever!
Luckily, I wasn't wearing it at the time.

Flash's letter:

Dear Mum,
We are doing water polo tomorrow! I bet I get the best ~~pony~~ polo pony 'cos I am certainly the best rider!
 Great nosh here! Piles of it! It's brilliant being with Eclaire and Lizzy! Lucky me!!
 X LOADS of LUV,
 X Mony X

Eclaire's letter:

Dear Mum and Dad,
 The food is measly, just a few specks. The bunks are teeny I keep falling OUT! A girl in our cabin cried all night long! otherwise it's lovely but I miss my ~~ck~~ cushions and my cuddly toys and my supper. Oh, and you!
Lots of L♥ve,
 X Eclairykins X X X X
 X   ♡ ♡

Lizzy's letter:

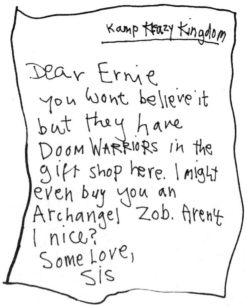

Kamp Krazy Kingdom

Dear Ernie
you wont believe it
but they have
DOOM WARRIORS in the
gift shop here. I might
even buy you an
Archangel Zob. Arent
I nice?
Some Love,
Sis

Owl felt quite cheery after writing her mean letter, but meanwhile, Eclaire had been hit by a huge wave of homesickness.

"Trouble is, I can't stand the grub," she said. "It's so unhealthy and the portions are tiny."

"Unhealthy?" chorused the other three, thinking of the vast amounts of sweeties and choccies they usually consumed in the company of Eclaire.

"And the beds are lumpy and teeeeeny. And Petula is a total drag. Urgh. Today's *abseiling*..."

"I think it's great," said Flash. "Hawkeye said I was the best archer he's ever had." Flash had already scored a record eight bullseyes with only ten arrows. And the camp leader, Big Chief Hawkeye, was, even Owl had to admit, probably the best-looking 25-year-old on the planet.

"You're not getting another *crush*, I hope," she said rather pompously.

Flash reddened and Lizzy speedily changed the subject.

"Do you know, I never thought I'd feel lonesome for my perfect brother, but I'm really missing old Ernie," Lizzy admitted. "And I can't believe we have to have a camp inspection every morning and make our beds. It's just like the army. And old Petula is such a cry baby."

"You ought to be n-nice to her," said Owl. "It's not much f-fun being with a group of girls who all hate you."

"But we did try," said Lizzy. "Eclaire offered her Nuclear Nougat, I offered to do her hair and Flash even tried to help her with the archery. But all she does is cry. It's pathetic."

That day, everything went from bad to worse for Owl. They played water polo (she could imagine Flash's embarrassed gloom when she discovered that it was, indeed, just standing waist-high in a pool and chucking a ball around), pass-over and chariot.

Owl seemed incapable of holding the ball for more than two seconds at a time. She remembered her first sewing lesson, when she was seven. Everyone else had finished sewing their little felt purses while she was still threading the needle.

"You're all fingers and thumbs," her teacher had said, and Owl had had a vision of a person with no arms and legs, just huge clumsy hands attached at four corners. That was how she felt now. Four big hands that couldn't catch. Bernice was everywhere, desperate to win, catching, shooting, diving, giving her all.

"Well played, Bernice," said Hawkeye. "You certainly stood up for your team." He then glanced in Owl's direction, with what she felt sure was a particularly ghastly mix of pity and scorn. If she could have slunk away and vanished from sight for ever, she would have done so then. It was unbearable.

Despite all Bernice's efforts, Apaches were

bottom of the league by the end of the day. Owl felt that it was all her fault.

At tea, Flash, Eclaire and Lizzy all agreed that they must do something to help Owl.

"Owly, there's something you'll be brilliant at, and it's worth a lot of points," said Flash.

"Oh, yes? What c-could that be? Slug imitations?" said Owl gloomily.

"No. Look," Lizzy waved the leaflet at Owl. "It's actually *two* things. *Quiz Evening* and *Talent Contest* – both on Thursday night."

Owl cheered up. Despite her extreme shyness in ordinary circumstances, she had discovered that on stage, all her nervousness evaporated. And quizzes were like falling off a log to her. Easy peasy.

"Yes!" shouted Flash. "You can do a rap song in the talent show! Eclaire can write it and I'll play drums."

"Fantastic," said Lizzy. "And do I get a look in?"

"Don't be daft," said Owl. "I'm in Apaches and y-you're in Mohicans. I'll have to do it with another Apache. Or on my own."

"Oh, yeah. Never mind. You'll be bound to win."

"But, how am I going to get through the next

f-few nights with the trio from hell?" sighed Owl.

"I've thought of that, too," said Flash. "Eclaire made the biggest batch of sweets *ever* today. Why don't you give them to those horrible old bats in your cabin as a peace offering?"

"Yeah," said Lizzy. "That should shut them up."

"I'll sacrifice my whole share to you," said Eclaire. "In fact, let's all sacrifice the whole lot."

"But we were going to have a midnight feast!" said Lizzy.

"N-no, I couldn't," whispered Owl, thinking of the midnight feast happening without her, while she lay lonely in her little bunk, being laughed at by Bernice and Co.

"Sorry," said Lizzy. "Of course you should have them all. Of course."

"Yup. Plenty more where they came from," said Eclaire, who was feeling considerably jollier, now that she had found a niche. She had been making sweets all afternoon in the kitchen, and had wangled a way to get points for creative cooking instead of for sport.

"Good old Eclaire," said Flash. "Somehow, she always finds a way to be happy against the odds."

Not like me, thought Owl, but she knew better than to say so and she was really pleased at the thought of the sweet horde. Surely that would win over the dreaded Bernice?

Sure enough, Sylvie and Mathadi were really nice to Owl when she dumped the vast sack of sweets on the cabin floor. And even Bernice allowed the hint of a grimace, that was almost a smile, to uncloud her bossy-boots mug.

She dived in and hurled four Karamel Kalashnikovs down her throat at once.

"Aaaaargh. Eough! Yeuk! Eeeeeeeeeeeeeeek! Water! Help!" she screamed.

Owl froze. What had gone wrong? Karamel Kalashnikovs were usually delicious. Surely Bernice was putting it on? But no, she was spitting and screaming.

The others were struck dumb, so Owl rushed to the basin, filled a glass, rushed back, tripped over the sack of sweets and gracefully emptied the whole glass of water over Bernice. The glass did a slow-motion somersault and smashed itself against the lamp, sending tiny shards of glass in all directions. Bernice screamed much louder and flailed about like a crab on its back.

"Don't move!" hissed Sylvie. "Glass!"

"Whassis, whassis, whassis?" came a familiar bellow. The cabin darkened as the gigantic frame of Mr Vim filled the far smaller frame of the cabin door.

"She's trying to kill me!" shrieked Bernice, waving her arms in Owl's direction. "I'm choking. I'm dying!" And she went into such a paroxysm of coughing and spluttering that even Mr Vim looked concerned for a millisecond. Then, he strode across the room, lifted the unfortunate Bernice by her heels and whacked her on the back. Two Karamel Kalashnikovs flew out of her mouth – splat! – against the cabin wall.

"Whassis, whassis, whassis?" thundered Vim, picking up the offending sweet sack. He popped a Kalashnikov into his cavernous mouth and let out a roar like the sound of two million buffalo snorting. A third Kalashnikov zoomed against the wall. *Sper-latt!*

"Whassis, whassis, whassis? That is the most disgusting thing I've ever had the displeasure of introducing to my *tongue*. Whoever bought this lot was robbed! Now clear up! Double quick! One-two one-two."

And Sylvie, Mathadi and Owl spent the next half an hour cleaning and hoovering and examining every inch of the cabin for minute slivers of glass, while Bernice got taken by Ironglove and Vim to the sick bay.

"S-sorry," said Owl eventually. "I-it must have been a b-bad batch. Eclaire... I mean Claire... usually makes the best sweets in the world."

"Rubbish," snorted Sylvie. "You were obviously trying to poison us."

"I wasn't! Look, I'll try one!" Needless to say,

after her taste of Kalashnikov, Owl performed the same manoeuvres as Bernice and Vim. Karamel Kalashnikov number four zoomed into the wall.

"Euuuugh." What had happened? Was this the Fab Four's idea of a joke? Owl was now even more miserable than before.

That night, her three room mates didn't talk to her at all. Apaches had had 30 points deducted from their score. They now had a pathetic 18 points and were bottom of the league. Comanches led with 106.

"Urgh. What a terrible day," said Bernice. "If only we had Pee-wee with us. She's such a good sport."

"Yeah, it would be great to have someone who *joins in* and doesn't give up under the slightest pressure. Never mind tries to poison you in their spare time."

"And loses you – how many points is it? Hmmm," said Bernice, counting up on her fingers. "I think Emily Smith has managed to lose us 30 points. And hasn't gained a single one for our team!" She glared at Owl, who was now curled up, pretending to be asleep.

"Yeah. And poor old Pee-wee says she's got three total wimps in with her."

A thought struck Owl. Who was this Pee-wee? She couldn't possibly be the self-same Petula who was driving the rest of the Fab Four mad – could she? *After all, Petula had said all her mates were at a different school, hadn't she?* But Petula was a total wimp, according to Flash, and the sporty Pee-wee didn't sound at all like the crybaby they described...

"Yeah," continued Sylvie. "She says one's got no money, one's got no brains and the other's so fat she keeps rolling off the bunk. It's like being in *The Wizard of Oz*. Ha ha ha!

Oh. It *is* them, thought Owl glumly. Petula's there and I'm here. Petula's really *Pee-wee* (must tell the others that!) and I'm really Owl. And we're *both* really miserable.

Bernice, Mathadi and Sylvie then had a pillow fight and a midnight feast, giggling hysterically and making nasty remarks about Owl until two in the morning. Owl didn't sleep a wink.

I'll have to get out of here, she thought. I can't stand it another second.

Six

The next morning, totally exhausted, Owl sneaked out to Mrs Ironglove's cabin at dawn.

"Emily. What's the matter, dear?" the drama teacher asked.

Owl was speechless. Mrs Ironglove sighed. Emily Smith was the shyest girl that she had ever come across. She had known plenty of shy children. There had been Damson, who went purple if anyone spoke to her, and Charlie, who stuttered so badly that he decided not to speak at all for a year.

And, of course, there was little Brian Hayseed, who went bright red if you looked at him and could quite easily be mistaken for a tomato. (It was best not to put him too close to a salad.)

But Emily seemed to be *incapable* of conquering her shyness. All the others had had their moments of happiness. But not Emily, except for that wonderful evening when she was in the school play... Sometimes, Mrs Ironglove herself thought Emily should be in a different school, but she didn't like to give up on her...

"Come on, Emily. What is it?"

"I w-want to go home. I'm s-sick."

Mrs. Ironglove felt Emily's forehead. "I don't think you're sick, Emily. You look perfectly fine to me."

"I can't s-sleep," muttered Owl. "I have not c-closed my eyes one single wink for this whole long and t-tormented night."

Mrs Ironglove smiled to herself. Emily, when she chose to, did have a way with words...

"Please, p-please Mrs Ironglove, can I s-sleep in your hut tonight? Please?"

"Look dear," said the teacher, "I think we should

give it one more night. Don't you like the girls in your cabin? I especially put you in with Sylvie and Mathadi because I thought they were kind girls."

"B-but B-Bernice—"

"Hmmm." Ironglove looked thoughtful. Then she looked a bit more thoughtful. Then she stroked her large crocodile chin with her vast claw. "I think I'll have a little word with Bernice," she croaked.

"Oh, no!" shouted Owl, so loudly that it was possible for Mrs Ironglove to hear her quite clearly. Ironglove felt quite dismayed and shocked.

"No. Pleeeeease don't do that," continued Owl. "I-I'd n-never hear the end of it."

They decided to give Owl one more night, and Ironglove agreed that if she couldn't sleep at all, she could stay with her the following night.

Owl felt a little relieved, but was dreading the day – a nightmarish vision of abseiling, white-water canoeing and a trip to the sand-bottling factory. She couldn't bear another sleepless night on top of this.

She scribbled a quick note to catch the morning post:

Dear Mum, Dad, and Loretta,

I am missing you all. I lied about the fried weasel. I lied about the safety helmets. I lied to give you a scare. It's actually much much worse than that. I am in a cabin with the trio from hell. They bully me all night long. I have now not slept a single wink for two whole nights. I am like Ophelia in the tower. Or Rapunzel or someone. Please rescue me. Please kiss Goldy for me. I hope he doesn't die of loneliness in the room by himself. Sorry, that smudge is a real tear.

Come and get me, pleeeeease. SOS.

Emily

She trailed back to her cabin, only to find that Hawkeye and White Dove were inspecting the bunks.

"Ten points off for a completely unmade bed, I'm afraid. A pity, when so many of the children are doing their very best.

"White Dove tutted as they left.

"Amazing, isn't it?" asked Bernice very loudly, "that some people can lose a whole 40 points, all by themselves?"

It was too much for Owl. She had promised herself she wouldn't do it, but it seemed that recently her promises had been made to be broken. She went to the pay phone and phoned home. She only meant to have a little chat (and a little cry), and get a little comfort from her only mother and sister and father in the whole wide world. She knew, somehow, that if she could just speak to her mum, everything would be all right.

But, of course, the answerphone was on. This sent Owl into floods of tears. If she could have just heard her mum's real voice, she was sure she would have been OK. As it was, she burst into tears and left the kind of message that every parent dreads, as follows:

"(sob sob) "Hello... It's me... (sob sob) Em... I... I... want...(sob sob)...to...come... home.(sob sob) Bye."

Owl felt much better - and much worse - when she'd made that call. She knew immediately how bad it would make her mother feel, but at the same time she felt relieved to have made it.

Oh dear, what a hopeless case I am, she thought. If only I had been in a cabin with the Fab Four, none of this would have happened.

Meanwhile, Eclaire, Lizzy and Flash had made an

interesting discovery. Thinking about what Owl had said, they had spent the night trying to be nice to Petula and had discovered the self-same thing that Owl had discovered. Petula was friends with Owl's arch enemies!

"Hey," said Flash. "I've got a great idea! Why don't we smuggle you over to their hut tonight?"

For the first time since she'd arrived at *Kamp Krazy Kingdom*, Petula cracked a smile. "You mean, do a swap?"

"Yeah. We'll alert Owly, I mean, Em, and she can be all ready to come back with us. The guard only wanders about every half hour, so we can be there and back in time to miss him, I bet. It'll probably only work for one night, but one night is better than none!"

"But they check the beds," said Eclaire.

"Me and Lizzy will go, and leave pillows in our bunks and Petula's, and you can answer for us in case anyone noses about."

"Brilliant," said Eclaire, resigned to the fact that it would take three pillows to look like her. Anyway, she would be the least nimble hurtling across the moors under cover of darkness. "It's a deal."

But at breakfast, Owl sat on her own and refused to come over to the Fab Four's table, even though they waved wildly at her.

Flash stomped over. "What's up?"

"Oh, n-nothing," said Owl, looking resolutely out of the window.

"Come on, spill the ketchup," said Eclaire, who had joined Flash.

"I suppose you think it was f-funny, trying to p-poison my cabin mates, but it's just m-made everything worse," mumbled Owl.

"What!!!!" shouted Flash and Eclaire so loudly that everyone looked up from their bowls of Buffalo Brownies.

Lizzy charged over to join them all.

"Shhhhh. We don't want to give the game away," she hissed, thinking they were discussing the Pee-wee-Owl swap.

"Owl said that we're trying to poison her," said Flash crossly.

"Oh, no!" said Eclaire, sitting down rather suddenly and missing the chair. The others pulled her to her feet. "Do you mean the Kalashnikovs?" she said.

"Of *course* I mean the Kalashnikovs. They were

poison. Bernice nearly choked and Vim nearly choked and..." Owl was furious.

Eclaire had a horrible realisation.

"Oh, no. I was in a real hurry when I made that batch. I thought I'd use that nice new jar of caster sugar, 'cos it would be smoother than granulated. But I must have used salt! Oh, Owlie, I'm soooooooooooo sorry."

Owl was won round eventually and, when they told her of the plan to swap her with Petula, she was positively jolly.

Meanwhile, Petula told Bernice, Mathadi and Sylvie about the plan and they all let out a loud cheer. Great, thought Owl. I may be glad to be leaving them, but I wish they weren't *quite* so pleased to be getting rid of me. Never mind. This evening she would be curled up alongside the Fab Four at last. Perhaps she would actually have a good night's sleep, too.

"It's the outing to sand-bottling factory today. Oh, what fun. I can hardly wait," carolled Bernice, pirouetting about the cabin and then, as usual, hogging the tiny mirror so that none of the others could do their hair. "Imagine all that sand going into all those little bottles. What overwhelming joy. Hooray, we are going with super duper Mr Vim, the loony, I mean, marvellous, PE teacher."

Sylvie and Mathadi were rolling about, kicking their legs in the air and laughing at Bernice. Owl thought that she would too, if Bernice was her friend. She had to admit that she could be quite funny...

"Now. *Be quiet* in the sand-bottling factory. They don't like *vibrations*," honked Mr Vim. He was an odd choice for this trip, thought Owl. His whisper was like a lovesick lion and even on tiptoe he trundled like a ten-tonne truck on tin cans.

The sand-bottling factory produced zillions of sweet little bottles of coloured sand in pretty patterns. You could even get someone's name written in sand. Owl was intrigued. They were obviously good presents and souvenirs of a happy time at *Kamp Krazy Kingdom – Where Adventure Never Ends.* (If you actually *had* had a happy time at *Kamp Krazy Kingdom – Where Adventure Never Ends,* that is...) When the Apaches arrived, everyone was eager to get points and started asking ridiculous questions to look keen.

"How many bits of sand go in each bottle?"

"How big is each particle of sand?"

"Do you make the sand pattern first and then make the bottle round it or the other way around?"

Mrs Stump, the poor woman who was leading the tour, blinked miserably and wished she was at home with a nice cup of tea in front of the telly.

"Or do you pick up each grain of sand with tweezers and paint it on its own?"

Eventually, even Bernice stopped thinking that this was funny and kicked Sylvie.

"Yeeough! Why did you do that?" screamed Sylvie much too loudly.

Mrs Stump cast a despairing look at Mr Vim.

"Minus five points, Apaches," he bellowed as softly as he could.

"Who's making that dreadful din?" asked a worried-looking overseer.

"Er... " honked Vim.

"I see," said the overseer, whose job it was to see, of course.

"Now, this splendid glass, sand and wotsit factory, provides essential jobs for the glass, sand and wotsit craftspeople who are natives of our lovely island," droned Mrs Stump, who had mouthed these very words six days a week for 25 summer seasons and 450 groups of schoolchildren. "I trust that when you all grow up to become upstanding members of your own society, even though most of you are unlucky enough to live in an urban nightmare and not on a lovely peaceful isle like our own, that you too will become involved in a profession that will bring joy and meaning to your lives, as you can see this does to our happy and fulfilled and, may I say, extremely talented, glass, sand and wotsit manufacturers. We are proud of our glass, sand and wotsits but we are proudest of all of the workpersonship and dexterity – if you haven't heard that word before, please look it up, that's what dictionaries are for – that goes into their making. Observe the fine handiwork and skill. Without the marvellous craftspersonship and industry of people like these, where would our nation be? At the bottom of the heap, that's where."

The children who hadn't dozed off during this speech looked around at the happy workforce. It seemed to Owl that a group of rather bored, sad-looking people were doing some rather dull things that looked a bit like what she used to do in Mrs Morbid's art class in the infants. But, since neither she nor anyone else wanted to lose any more points, nobody disagreed with Mrs Stump.

After an astonishingly unpleasant packed lunch, provided by White Dove, who would, thought Owl, be better off as a prison guard than trying to do anything with kids, it was time to go on the island's famous chair lift.

"I would like you to examine the mechanism of this marvellous chair lift," trilled Mrs Stump, clearly relieved to be free of the sand-bottling factory. "It will take you floating high above the glorious scenic scenery of our lovely island. Observe the sparkling spindles, the exquisite threddles, the luminous boingles... Without all this, where would our industry be? Perhaps we would not even be blessed with the simple teacup!"

The girls and boys thought how sad it would be not to have a teacup. At least, they looked as if they were thinking this. Even Mr Vim thought that Mrs Stump might possibly have thought of something more likely to capture the children's imagination, but he let it pass.

"The simple teacup?" asked Bernice. "Would we also be short of other interesting things, like teaspoons, bits of fluff, or perhaps, toenail clippers?"

Mr Vim glared at her. Everyone, even Owl, giggled.

But it was lost on Mrs Stump. "Yes, yes, my dear. Imagine a world without those things! Now, who would like to go first on the chair lift?"

A flurry of hands went up. Owl's was not among them.

"I always like to choose a person who doesn't push themselves forward. How about you?" commanded Mrs Stump, grasping Owl's hand. Owl could hear her room mates groaning. "And you, dear." To Owl's horror, Mrs Stump picked Bernice. "Shy girl and confident girl. Always a good combination. The one will look after the other."

Owl gulped. She didn't want to go on the chair lift. Not at all. It looked very high and very scary. Owl did not have a good head for heights. She didn't even like her bunk bed that much. She had been pleased when Bernice and Sylvie nabbed the top bunks in the cabin. She had only agreed to a bunk bed at home because her room was so small that she couldn't fit a desk in otherwise.

The thought of being up in the air with her tormentor was absolutely terrifying.

"Isn't it a bit w-wet?" she tried to squeak. But her mouth had gone completely dry and even her usual tiny voice was muffled. Not a peep came out.

Bernice threw her an evil stare. "Oh, well. If I must," she said.

Before she knew it, Owl was sitting in the little iron chair with Bernice, the machinery was cranking and the chair was rising. Up, up, up they went. And down, down, down came the pouring rain.

"Did you know that you can raise this bar?" said Bernice, jiggling the bar that Owl was gripping onto for dear life. "You could raise it, then you could give the person next to you a little push and they would *plummet like a stone* into the abyss..."

Owl made a mistake. She looked down. She felt a horrible lurching inside her stomach that rushed up her throat, sped to her head and settled on her chest. She was too frightened even to be sick. She clenched her fists tightly round the bar and stared ahead, trying to think of something else. Anything. She concentrated on the carpet in her bedroom, which was blue with multicoloured dots. She tried to count the dots.

"Did you hear what I said?" whispered Bernice, menacingly.

Owl opened her mouth. "28," she squeaked.

"What?" shouted Bernice.

"29, 30..." said Owl, robotically, staring ahead, her brain whirling.

Bernice pulled at the bar and, to Owl's horror, her own grip weakened by terror, the bar sprung up! The chair lift was at its highest point. There was absolutely nothing to stop the two of them falling out and down, down, down...
Bernice shrieked, lurched and grabbed Owl's arm. Owl snatched upwards at the bar and pulled it down. *Slam!* The seat swung and wobbled and they were gliding down to safety.

"I didn't think it would go up. I thought it had a safety lock," whispered Bernice.

Owl stared ahead. "31,32..."

When they got to the ground, both girls were violently sick.

Even Mr Vim needed a sit down after that. Of course, he deducted 40 points from Apaches and banned Bernice and Owl from any activities for the rest of the day. Yippee, thought Owl. No white-water canoeing. No abseiling. And tonight she would be with the Fab Four. She was so relieved to be alive, she didn't even feel angry with Bernice. Anyway, she'd noticed two things. Bernice had clung onto Owl. Owl wasn't sure why, but she felt that Bernice had been trying to stop Owl from falling. She had also, Owl knew, not meant to lift the bar. She had almost, *almost* said sorry. It would do.

They were allowed to visit the souvenir shop before going back to camp. Owl bought a bottle of sand with MUM written in red sand, a fake leather bookmark with DAD on and a keyring marked LAURA. It was annoying, you could never get anything with LORETTA on. She had 20p left, but was hardly in the mood for sweets. The journey back to camp was very quiet indeed.

Seven

Things were very quiet in Owl's cabin that night. Apaches were now actually *minus* points. This was unheard of in the whole history (ten years) of *Kamp Krazy Kingdom – Where Adventure Never Ends.*

What's more, although Owl seemed to have lost zillions of points herself, It had been Bernice's crazed behaviour on the chair lift that caused them to plummet below zero. Bernice was unusually quiet and complained of not feeling well.

"At least we'll have Petula tonight," ventured Mathadi.

"And lose even more points," muttered Sylvie, "for smuggling cabin mates."

"Oh, who cares about stupid points?" said Bernice angrily. "You obviously didn't or you wouldn't have asked all those daft questions."

"*You* were the one who cared!" retorted Sylvie.

"You said that if we had Petula, we would win! Instead of stupid old Emily."

Silence greeted this remark. But Owl was so excited at the thought of being smuggled to the Fab Four's cabin that she couldn't care less.

"There's 50 points for the *Quiz* and 60 points for the *Talent Contest* winner – we might get one of those," mumbled Sylvie, to a stony silence.

Meanwhile, Lizzy and Flash and Petula were plotting their escape. They shoved pillows and clothes into their beds, as Eclaire looked gloomily on, wishing, not for the first time that week, that she was just a tiny bit, well, not slimmer – she couldn't bear all that junk about skinny women – but perhaps, well, fitter. It would have been fun to do a bit more sport and, frankly, she had almost seen enough of the kitchen to put her off cooking for ever. It would, she admitted to herself, have been nicer to have decided who would go with Petula by drawing straws or eeny-meeny-miny-mo or tossing a coin or something, instead of everyone immediately assuming that she wouldn't want a physical adventure...

Flash, meanwhile, was enjoying herself.

"Right. Torch, map, compass, bottle of water, spare socks..."

"Flash, this is a 500-metre walk, not a polar expedition," said Eclaire grumpily.

"You can never be over-prepared," said Flash. "It's been raining for a day and a half and the ground's soggy."

"Also, we could, well, take a wrong turning," mumbled Lizzy, gazing doubtfully at the camp map, which showed a straight line between their hut and Owl's.

"Yes," said Petula, sounding quite chirpy for once. "And we'll have to dodge the guards."

"Anyone would think it was the SAS, not a bunch of students on their first job," huffed Eclaire. "Those 'guards', as you call them, are about Loretta's age."

"Look Eclairykins, I know you're sorry not to come, but you'll be performing the vital task of holding the fort for us. If any nosey parkers come round, you have to make sure they don't prod our beds!"

"I'm not sorry. I'm fine," snorted Eclaire.

"Shhhhhh!" A beam of torchlight shone through the cabin's window and Flash ducked. "Guards patrolling."

They all held their breath. Two minutes later, Flash, Lizzy and Petula snuck out and darted behind the nearest cabin. The camp was eerily quiet. Flash's plan had been to sneak from cabin to cabin until they had cleared the Mohicans camp, then run across the wide area, skirting round the Comanches camp, where it was most likely the guards could spot them. Then they only had to go very carefully past the main teachers' huts and bingo! They'd be at the Apaches camp.

It was a wild and stormy night and the rain was driving down like icicles... They fell in two ditches and poor old Petula dropped her rucksack, containing all her stuff, into a deep muddy trench. As they were hunting for it, a torch beam shone straight towards them.

They dived into the ditch face-down in the icy mud and the beam shone straight above their heads.

"Who goes there?" asked a high voice.

The three girls lay as still as statues, listening to the tramp and squelch of two grumpy guards' feet sloshing towards them.

"Probably a rabbit," said one.

"Yeah, no one's gonna come out in this weather. Let's get back in the hut," said the other.

And, to the girls' relief, they retreated.

"Right, let's make a dash for it," whispered Flash.

They staggered out of the ditch and hared towards the Apaches encampment, making a wide berth round the huts containing Vim and Co.

"Right, this is it," said Flash confidently. And she made the low hooting noise that she had agreed with Owl.

"Whatever's that? An owl?" came an extraordinary croaking sound that sent a chill down the trio's backs. It was, of course, the voice of Mrs Ironglove, which, as none of them attended Owl's school, they'd never had the pleasure of hearing before.

"Quick! Down!" hissed Flash and they ducked out of sight just as the Ironglove came to her window with her binoculars.

"Oh, well. I shan't see it in this awful storm," creaked Ironglove. "Do you think it could have been an Owl, Mrs Spindle?"

"That, or a lesser-spotted ganymede warbler," squeaked the Spindle.

It was all Flash and Lizzy could do not to explode with laughter. Petula stifled a squeak.

"Yes, I do believe it *is* a lesser-spotted ganymede. Oh, Vera, *do* let's look. That would be so exciting. I haven't heard one of those since I was a girl. You know they do that strange hoot followed by a squeak. We could write to *Ornithologists' Weekly* and we might get a prize!"

The girls could hear the two teachers pulling on some clothes. They were actually going to come out and search for the lesser-spotted ganymede warbler! They were obviously mad, thought Lizzy. What self-respecting bird would be warbling and hooting after midnight on a stormy night?

"Run!" she hissed. And without thinking what they were doing, the girls hurtled off.

Much more by luck than judgement, the first cabin they came to was Owl's. She had, as agreed, pinned a note to the door saying "THIS ONE". They didn't stop, or even bother about being quiet any more, but banged on the door.

A ruffled Bernice opened it.

"Shhhh. Why on earth are you making such a *din*?"

"Quick, hide us. The teachers are coming."

Hiding three extra girls in a small cabin built for four is no easy task.

Lizzy was furious to find that Owl was curled up fast asleep on the bottom bunk.

"I thought she couldn't sleep a wink!" she snorted.

"You'll all just have to squash into the loo!" whispered Bernice. "And I'll come in too."

Flash wondered why, but she didn't have time to think it over, because, sure enough, Ironglove was tapping on the door.

"Is anyone awake in there?" she called.

"Only me!" shouted Bernice. "I'm in the loo."

"Sorry, dear, but we thought we saw someone coming into the hut," said the drama teacher.

"Oh, no," said Bernice. "It's just the three of us."

Ironglove came in anyway and shone her torch on the three apparently sleeping girls. Something, she felt, was not quite right. Why were they so fast asleep despite her banging on the door and shouting? She approached the loo door.

"Are you all right, Bernice?"

"Ooh. No. I've got a stomach upset."

"Oh, you poor dear," said Mrs Ironglove in her best dragon tones. "I'll just wait here until you come out to make sure you're OK."

"Ooh, no, Mrs Ironglove, don't you worry about that. I'll be just fine," squeaked Bernice, who was finding it difficult to talk at all, seeing as Flash's elbow was stuck against her jaw and Petula was virtually sitting on her head. Poor Lizzy was squished so hard between the tiny sink and the loo that she could barely breathe. The loos were built for one person, naturally.

"All right, dear," said Ironglove, not wanting to embarrass the poor, sick girl. "I'll come and check in half an hour."

But the sigh of relief from inside the loo was so loud that Mrs Ironglove's suspicions were further alerted. She and Mrs Spindle hovered outside the hut until they heard a very strange noise.

Ironglove opened the door as fast as a shark swooping on a minnow and saw a most interesting sight. The door of the loo had burst open and an extraordinary creature, waving slimy tentacles, matted in mud, lay squirming on the floor. Mrs Spindle emitted the kind of scream you usually only hear in films where lonely heroines go over the moors with nothing to protect them but a guttering candle.

"EEEEEEEEEEEEEEEEEEEEEEEEEEEEEEEEEEEK!"

Lights went on all over the camp. People came running from all directions.

The first to arrive was Mr Vim. Anyone who hadn't been woken up by the shrill scream of Mrs Spindle was certainly alerted by Vim's roar.

"Whassis, whassis, whassis?!!!" he raged.

The slimy creature squirmed and revealed itself to be a tangle of girls, covered almost completely in mud. Flash, Petula, Lizzy and the slightly less muddy Bernice emerged.

"Whoopsy," said Owl, sitting up with a start and banging her head on the cabin roof. Which only showed, she thought later, how extremely small those cabins were.

Eight

The next morning, Owl woke up feeling as if her head had been chewed by a bear. Flash had been absolutely brilliant the night before, no doubt about it. She had said, as soon as she had gathered her wits, which, being Flash, was very quickly indeed, that all they had been going to do was have a midnight feast. Midnight feasts, although frowned upon, were not so very uncommon and it sounded a lot better than admitting they were smuggling Petula out to swap her with Owl.

Even so, Apaches had lost a further 20 points and Mohicans had lost 40! So both her own team and her best friends' team were losers and it was all her fault.

The only person who woke up happy was Mrs Ironglove. She chuckled at the thought of Mrs Spindle and the monster. She remembered her own midnight feasts as a girl. But, secretly, she was most pleased to find that Emily's friends had come to have a midnight feast with her. Emily did have some friends after all! Mrs Ironglove had thought that Emily would be spending the night with her that night and she always felt it was rather an admission of failure to have to remove a child.

Meanwhile, Mathadi, Sylvie and Bernice were whispering together.

"Well, she must be OK, if she's got mates who are prepared to come out in this weather to rescue her and help Pee-wee," said Sylvie.

"Yeah. And we must be pretty horrible for her to want to be rescued so much," said Mathadi.

Bernice kept a stony silence.

Mathadi and Sylvie decided to make it up to Owl at breakfast, but Owl would not play ball.

"Look, my friends didn't like Petula much, but they weren't horrible to her, like you were to me," she said.

"You're right," said Mathadi. "We just wanted to impress Bernice, you know, because she's..."

"A b-bossy know-it-all?" said Owl.

"I guess so," admitted Mathadi.

"Right," said Owl. "We've got two w-ways to do well today. We've got the *Quiz* and the *Talent Show.* I'm, er, quite g-good at quizzes, so I'll be team captain if you like."

"But Bernice is doing it! She's the best of us. And she'll never want you to..."

"I don't care," said Owl, with new confidence. "I know I can win a quiz. Each school is only allowed two teams, and I know who the other team leader should be."

"Well, it'll have to be Bernice. If we back you up, she'll go ballistic," said Sylvie.

"I think it's t-time we stood up to her," said Owl, amazed at her firmness.

"But who else would you want? Bernice is really clever! And you can't have your friends, 'cos they're in Mohicans."

"I have got another friend, actually," said Owl.

"Who?"

"Brian Hayseed."

"Brian Hayseed? He wouldn't say boo to a goose!"

Owl knew that. People had always told her that she wouldn't say boo to a goose herself. That she wouldn't even say boo to a worm. That if an ant was approaching her sandwich, she wouldn't have the courage to shoo it away. But she had seen little Brian Hayseed sitting alone at every single meal all week and she had been too excited by her chance to talk to the Fab Four, which she only got at mealtimes, to do anything about it. Now was her chance to make things good for Brian, as well as for herself.

"Brian Hayseed will be fine," she said.

But Sylvie and Mathadi were still under Bernice's thumb. They couldn't bring themselves to stand up to her.

"Hmm," said Owl to herself. "This looks like a job for the Fab Four."

At lunch, Owl made a beeline for Brian Hayseed. "Brian! Haven't seen you all w-week!" she lied.

Brian's little round face lit up and he gazed at Owl as though she were an ice-cream mountain.

"Where have y-you *been* all week?" exclaimed Owl, not wanting him to see that she knew he had been sitting alone pretending to read his book every meal time.

"Oh. Um," said Brian articulately.

"Well, never mind, I've f-found you at *last*. And I'm really glad!"

While all the tables were being organised for the *Quiz Evening* (to be followed by the *Talent Contest*), Flash, Lizzy and Eclaire zapped into action.

"Bernice," wheedled Eclaire. "You're just *exactly* the person we need to help with the *Talent Contest* catering. I gather it was *you* who immediately identified my foolish substitution of sugar with salt. Silly me!"

"Pull the other one," huffed Bernice, smelling a rat. "I can't boil an egg."

"Can't you?" said Eclaire, all wide-eyed innocence. "I *am* surprised."

"You can't have her helping you," chipped in Flash. "I need her to work out the table plan. You see it's quite complicated... we have to have different teams on each table, so one lot of Apaches can't help the other lot. But then if they're all sitting too close to each other, it could get awkward..."

"What are you asking me for?" sniffed Bernice, "The teacher should be organising that sort of thing. I didn't come here to shift chairs. Anyway, I'm *doing* the *quiz*."

"Yes, but we've all got to muck in," said Flash, with a mischievous twinkle. "You know, team spirit."

"Oh, *poo* to team spirit," snorted Bernice. "I'm here to win."

"You don't believe in *team spirit*?" said Flash, extremely loudly. "Well... I *am* surprised."

"Of *course* she does, don't you, Bernice," said Lizzy. "She's on the rota to come and help with the lighting for the talent contest."

"Rota? What rota?" asked Bernice, visibly rattled.

"You volunteered," said Lizzy, waving a piece of paper in front of Bernice's nose. "That shows that you care about the Greater Good."

"I did *not* volunteer," said Bernice, snatching the piece of paper and peering at it. It was, in fact, an excellently forged rota that Lizzy had done that morning.

"But I don't know *anything* about lights!"

shouted Bernice. "And I can't do it at three o'clock. That's when the quiz starts."

"You don't know anything about lights? Well why did you put your name down?" asked Lizzy, with a cherubic smile.

Right on cue, Owl came over and piped up. "Actually, Bernice, I've been voted, um, to be the Apache t-team leader for the quiz. And Brian is to be my deputy."

"Whaaaat?" shouted Bernice, so everybody turned to look. "But I'm doing it. I've always been going to do it!"

"Who voted for you?" asked Lizzy innocently.

"Nobody, I mean... But I'm the best!"

"Best at what?" asked Eclaire, sweetly. "Obviously not cooking."

"And clearly not team spirit."

"And no good on lighting," added Lizzy.

"Well, of course I'm doing it, aren't I Sylvie?" huffed Bernice, turning round to look for her friends. "Sylvie...? Mathadi?"

But Sylvie and Mathadi were nowhere to be seen.

Bernice then had a very unusual experience. She

felt a tear welling up in the corner of one eye. And then in the corner of the other.

"Oh, Bernice, sorry," whispered the good-natured Owl, who did feel genuinely sorry for her.

"Shut up. I've just got an allergy," said Bernice. "An allergy to you." And she stormed out. The Fab Four looked at each other guiltily.

"Oh, dear," said Eclaire. "Maybe we shouldn't have locked Sylvie and Mathadi in the cupboard."

"What?" gasped Owl.

"Well, we thought they might back up Bernice," said Flash guiltily.

"What do you mean, 'we'?" asked Lizzy angrily. "You never told me!"

"Well," blushed Eclaire. "We didn't really plan it. It's just that Mathadi and Sylvie were passing the sports equipment cupboard...and..."

Flash butted in, "And we heard them saying that they couldn't let Owl do the quiz because Bernice would be so upset."

"And we just sort of instinctively ran up and gave them a little push and, before we knew it, they'd, well, fallen into the cupboard and..."

"So we locked the door," concluded Flash. "It's all right though. They didn't know it was us!"

"What do you mean, all right?" shouted Lizzy. "They could suffocate!"

"Don't be stupid. It's a little room, really, not a cupboard... Sorry, Owl. We did it for you..."

But Owl was already halfway across the field towards the sports storeroom.

She had unbolted the door and was busy apologising to Sylvie and Mathadi by the time the rest of the Fab Four arrived.

To their amazement, Sylvie, Mathadi and Owl were all giggling.

When they'd heard about Bernice's stroppy behaviour, Mathadi and Sylvie had been quite relieved not to be dragged further into all her troubles.

Owl and Brian scored 98 out of 100 in the quiz. For coming first, Apaches got 50 points.

The team scores now stood at:

Comanches 102

Mohicans 98

Apaches -2

"Well," muttered Owl, whose strong point was not maths. "Even I know that's b-better than -52."

Brian and Owl were carried around the hall on the shoulders of whooping Apaches.

"All we have to do now is come first and second in the talent contest! Whoopeeeeee! Owl will easily win that!" shouted Mathadi.

"Not if I have anything to do with it!" came a familiar voice.

Owl froze.

Surely that was... it couldn't be... could it?

Yes. It was her mum. "Goodness me. And I thought you were at death's door! Have you dragged me all the way here for nothing?"

"Mum, I c-c-can explain everything!"

"Yes. I think you have a *lot* of explaining to

do, young lady. But first, I want you to take me to the camp office, so they can explain to me why they haven't got the proper safety equipment..."

And Mrs Smith swooped out of the hall, with Owl trailing quavering in her wake.

As soon as they were outside, Owl dragged her mother to one side.

"We c-can't go to the office, Mum. It was all a lie."

"What?"

"Of course they have all the right stuff. I-I just wanted to get you to get me away from here. And then when I left that last message... things were really bad..." Owl's voice trailed away. "B-but I never thought you would actually come here... Why didn't you *ring*?"

"I tried to ring. It would have helped if you had given me the right telephone number. When I finally did get the number, the teacher said that you were rather miserable, but she was sure you would cheer up. Then I got that last message and I couldn't get through again, so I just came down. I was soooo worried!"

"Oh, Mum. I'm soooo sorry."

"Well, sorry's no good. Pack your bag now and we can get the four o'clock ferry."

"But I'll miss the *T-talent C-contest.*"

"And the flying pigs."

Owl went glumly to her cabin to pack.

Meanwhile Mrs Ironglove invited Mrs Smith for a cup of tea.

And a little chat. The little chat was about how Owl's confidence had improved so much during the week. And how very good it would be for her to have a go in the Talent Contest. And about what a shame it would be if she had to go home before all the other girls. And how there was a spare bunk in the teachers cabin that Mrs Smith could sleep in if she liked, and it wasn't very comfy but wouldn't it be rather fun to see all the children in the talent show? And how the teachers really could do with a bit of help since poor Mr Vim had lost his voice on account of a little incident the night before...

When Owl returned with her bag, her mum had given in. She was secretly pleased that Emily seemed to have gained so much confidence. She had been thrilled to see her carried round the camp on everyone's shoulders when she arrived. But she wasn't going to admit that to Emily.

"Mrs Ironglove has asked me to stay on and help, since Mr Vim has lost his voice. So you'll just have to stay another night, whether you like it or not."

Whoooopeee, thought Owl. "Oh. OK," is what she said.

And she rushed off to put her name down for the talent show.

Ten

Owl stared at the *Talent Show* programme pinned to the notice board:

KAMP KRAZY KINGDOM

 Proudly Presents
GRAND TALENT SHOW

Compered by BRIAN ('Brain') HAYSEED
and PETULA ('Personality') PARKINSON
Featuring:
Carlos, the miniature rapper (Comanches)
Rufus, the human beat box (Apaches)
Lisa the snake girl (Mohicans)

 INTERVAL

Elastic Flash (Mohicans)
The Great Adamski (Comanches)
Bernice Berens sings the blues (Apaches)

Owl gulped in dismay. She was too late to sign up.

"Look!" she called to the Fab Four. "Look!"

"What's up? It looks great," said Flash, who was quite pleased with her billing.

"What's up?" said Owl. "I'm not in the p-programme. *That's* what's up!"

"Oh, my Lord," said Eclaire. "Bernice has gone and put herself in instead of you!"

"Exactickly," said Owl. "And she can't sing for t-toffee. She sounds like a parrot with a mouthful of f-fudge."

"How do you know she can't sing?" demanded Eclaire.

"She used to sing in the loo. And, honestly, it's like listening to a t-turkey drowning in glue. Really."

"This looks like a case for the Fab Four," said Lizzy – and they hurtled to Owl's cabin to confront Bernice.

But Bernice was nowhere to be found.

"Oh noooo!" Owl was beginning to panic, "My mum is only staying 'cos I was in the concert. She came all this way to rescue me, and then

Ironglove persuaded her to stay to see the show and now..."

"Look, Bernice can't just go and put herself down like that. I mean, you got chosen."

"I suppose Bernice is trying to get back at you for stealing her quiz off her," said Lizzy. "Maybe she has a point."

"Traitor," said Flash. "How can anyone have a point against a member of the Fab Four?"

"YES. Rrrrrrrrrrrrright," growled Lizzy. "How could I forget?"

"Four for one and one for four
Funny, clever, rich and poor
Frizzy, Flash, Eclaire and Owl
Stick together, fair or foul.

"All for one and one for all
Fatty, skinny, short and tall
Frizzy, Flash, Owl and Eclaire
Stick together, foul or fair."

"So, for the honour of the Fab Four, we have to track down Bernice and lock her in the sports cupboard. *And* we have to reprint the programmes. Quick!"

Eclaire wrote out Owl's name and taped it over Bernice's. Then she went to the staff room and asked to photocopy some more programmes, because not enough seemed to have been printed.

Luckily, Mr Vim was in charge, and was sitting, a shadow of his former self, with a muffler around his throat and hugging a hot-water bottle.

Obviously, the Karamel Kalashnikovs had combined with the Stormy Night of the Slimy Monster to wreck even Mr Vim's shouting power.

"Please, Mr Vim," Eclaire wheedled. "We've only got eight programmes for some reason and we need lots more."

Mr Vim nodded pathetically.

Eclaire couldn't think why everyone in Owl's school was so scared of him. 'He's a pussy cat,' she thought.

Of course, Eclaire's version of the programme didn't look that great, even she had to admit.

Here it is:

KAMP KRAZY KINGDOM

Proudly Presents
GRAND TALENT SHOW

**Compered by BRIAN ('Brain')HAYSEED
and PETULA ('Personality') PARKINSON
Featuring:
Carlos, the miniature rapper (Comanches)
Rufus, the human beat box (Apaches)
Lisa the snake girl (Mohicans)**

INTERVAL

**Elastic Flash (Mohicans)
The Great Adamski (Comanches)
Emily Smith (Apaches)
COSTUMES: Claire. DRUMS: Lizzy
LIGHTS: Flash. (ALL from the
FAB MOHICANS!**

When Owl saw it, her heart sank. A handwritten name did not look great compared to a nicely printed stage name, like all the others. And she felt slightly embarrassed that Claire had drawn attention to herself and Lizzy as well.

"Look, we need to give the Mohicans a boost,"

said Eclaire. "And we have done more than the others. Flash rigged up all the lights!"

Owl agreed, but she had a sinking feeling. Where was Bernice?

However, the next half hour was really fun. The Fab Four, and, to Owl's great delight, Sylvie, Mathadi and Brian, all helped her and Flash to get ready for the *Talent Show*. Flash, who was doing her human contortionist act, had a flashy leotard covered in gold stars. Ironglove, kindly as ever, had provided a dressing-up box for the occasion and eventually they found a brightly-coloured flowery dress and a pink sparkly cardigan for Owl to wear. Mathadi dabbed on a bit of glitter, rouge and lipstick and stepped back to admire her handiwork.

"Owly, you look like Cinderella," breathed Mathadi.

"Before or after the b-ball?" giggled Owl, quite pleased with the effect. "Have you, er, seen Bernice?" she added, worried.

"Oh, yeah. She's in the sick room with Mrs Spindle and Mr Vim."

"Serves her right. Who cares?" shouted everyone else.

'I do,' thought Owl. 'Something's going to happen...'

And she was right.

Eleven

"Now peoples, I gon tell you what to do
if you don fancy goin on white-water canoe
an the thought of chair lift make you blue.
Then here's a trick to fool the rest
and mek dem tink you are the best.
If abseiling ain't quite your ting
jus slip your arm into a sling
jus say you can't do any ting.
You's Olympic material most of the time
there is no mountain you can't climb
but you done gone and broke you arm
(saving some kid from terrible harm).
So you is very sad to say
you is just gonna have to pass today.
Then you sits back and gets a chance to chill
while Krazy Kamp ragamuffins climb that hill
and swim that swim and do that ting.
See? All you need is a neat arm sling."

"Why didn't I think of that?" Owl whispered to Flash, as Carlos the miniature rapper exited to wild applause.

"Yes. It would have *really* suited Eclaire," agreed Flash, who was feeling a little embarrassed at the thought of her contortionist act.

"How old is that kid anyway? He looks about six. He's brilliant."

"Size doesn't matter," hissed Carlos, who had sneaked up behind them before taking his encore. "Does it?" he winked at Owl, who was a centimetre shorter.

"No offence," said Flash.

"None taken." And Carlos leaped back on stage to rousing cheers.

"Well, he'll win. And he's in Comanches," said Owl flatly, although she was secretly feeling that she might have a new friend in Carlos, who lived over the road from her and had never even looked at her before.

Owl enjoyed the talent contest, although she had to admit that the first two acts were a lot better than she had hoped. Carlos and Rufus, the human beat box, both sounded like they were ready to accept recording contracts. But Lisa the Snake Girl cheered Owl up by rising slinky and snake-like from a basket to Indian music, then sticking her tongue out, squeaking in horror and collapsing straight back into the basket in tears.

"Oh no, her forked tongue fell off," whispered a sympathetic Flash.

"That's no reason to give up," hissed Brian as poor Lisa slithered offstage wailing.

During the Interval, Owl felt sick. It was stage fright, she knew, but she had only been on stage once before and this suddenly seemed horribly important. After all, her first appearance had only been understudying a tree stump...

Then, to her horror, she found that she had hiccups.

"You need water," said Brian, who knew all about being sick during school plays.

"Drink it backwards," urged Flash.

"Count to two thousand, holding your breath," said Carlos wickedly.

"Put your head between your knees and say the alphabet backwards," piped up Mathadi.

"Whose side are you – HIC – on?" snarled Owl.

"Well, don't stand in the wings. Everyone'll hear you. And that will certainly ruin *my* act," hissed the Great Adamski, who was, Owl reflected, quite extraordinarily tall all of a sudden, and draped in an impressive black cloak from head to foot.

Owl mooched further backstage, accompanied by an anxious Brian.

"Good – HIC – luck, then," she spluttered to Flash.

Petula announced, "And now, the marvellous, the wondrous, the rubber-limbed Elastic Flash!" and Flash cart-wheeled into the spotlight.

Flash did amazing contortions and ended up with her feet round her neck, having to be untangled by Lizzy. Still, she got a generous round of applause.

The Great Adamski met an even worse fate, however. Everyone gasped in awe as the unusually tall figure of the magician glided on stage.

"From zis hat," he drawled, in a fake Italian accent, "I shall draw not one, not two, but threeeeeeeeee rabeeets."

He swept the top hat off his head and, sadly, all three rabbits flew out over the heads of the audience. One was Owl's little pink and yellow rabbit and one was Brian's!

"You've nicked our rabbits!" shrieked Brian, before he had time to check himself. There was a roar of laughter and poor Adamski teetered and crashed to the floor.

"So that's why he was so – HIC – tall, HIC! He was on stilts!"

"I'll never live this down," said poor Brian.

"Neither will – HIC – he," said Owl. "Anyway, no one will know it was – HIC - you that shouted. You're back here with – HIC – me."

"So I am," said Brian, a smile too big for his little face crossing it like sunshine after rain.

"Hmmm. Things are looking up. You've got a chance of coming third after Carlos and Rufus," calculated Brian cheerfully.

"HIC!" said Owl, as, she realized that it was her turn. She was next!

It was Brian's turn to announce Owl, but, as he walked on, to a roll of drums (Lizzy on cake tins), he was surprised to see Petula flouncing on from the opposite side.

"It's my turn," Brian hissed, but Petula started her announcement unperturbed, so he just joined in.

Together, Brian and Petula announced:

"And as the finale of our wonderful talent show here at the *Kamp Krazy Kingdom – Where Adventure Never Ends*, Apaches present the very wonderful, the very fabulous, the very marvelous..."

And then Brian said, "EMILY SMITH", but Petula said, at exactly the same moment, "BERNICE BERENS singing the BLUES."

As Owl walked on stage from the right, Bernice entered from the left! Owl stood blinking, dazzled by the spotlights. Bernice had found a dazzling blue dress with silver stars. She looked about two metres tall. The Apaches were all cheering. No one had expected a double act. Bernice started to sing.

Her voice was like syrup. Honey. Nightingales. Skylarks. Opera divas. Choir boys.

"Born under a baaaaaaaaad star
been saaaaaaaaad since I was small" (here she threw a withering look at Owl)
"If it wasn't for baaaaaaaaaaaaaaad luck
I wouldn't have no luck at all!"

.

The hall was completely silent, enthralled by Bernice.

Owl couldn't believe the difference in Bernice's voice. She knew she had only two choices: flight or fight. She glanced behind her. She could see, in the wings, the anguished frozen faces of Lizzy, Brian and worse, her mum. She could imagine the expressions of Eclaire and Flash, sitting in the audience. And so, although frozen with terror, she chose. Fight. She would turn this into a duet.

She swayed up to Bernice, hoping her wobbly walk would look like an elegant sashay, and, smiling what she hoped was a dazzling smile, she improvised:

"Yeah, you was born under a baaaaaaaaaad star
You was down since you could crawl
But it wasn't for the likes of meeeeeeeee
You wouldn't have no luck at aaaaaaaaaaaaaall!"

Bernice gawped at Owl. She hadn't heard Owl sing before. She had no idea how good she was. Owl gaped back. Of course, they had heard each other humming a bit in the cabin, when they just sounded like anyone else. This was very different. Bernice's voice certainly didn't sound like it had in the loo! They gawped some more. This was a moment that seemed like an hour to the two girls (but it was only a few seconds to the audience), when the whole of the last week flashed before them. The Kalashnikovs, the slime monster, the chair lift.

Then, as Lizzy cleverly drummed another roll on the biscuit tins, Owl tentatively offered Bernice her hand. Lizzy stopped in mid drumroll. You could hear a feather fall.

Bernice turned away, then turned back to Owl and took her hand.

"And now, for our final number," said Owl, as

though they had rehearsed it a thousand times: "The duetting Apaches, Bernice and Emily, will sing, er..." She pretended to cough, put her hand in front of her face and whispered, "What shall we sing?"

"Summertime," said Bernice confidently.

So they did.

"Summertime and the living is easy..."

When they finished, the hall erupted.

They won, with 60 points each!! Rufus the human beat box was second, with 50 points, so since he was an Apache too, Apaches got 170 points in the talent contest alone.

Which meant they stormed into the lead with 108 points!

Owl glanced at Bernice, who was glancing at Owl. They both looked away very quickly. Then they looked at each other again. And then a smile hovered on Bernice's grumpy mug and then it decided to stop hovering and break into a huge grin. And Owl felt exactly the same thing happening to her face and had an extraordinarily strong desire to hug Bernice very hard. But Bernice was giving her her a high-five instead.

YES! And before they knew it, Big Chief Hawkeye and an unusually smiling White Dove were giving them a big silvery cup. And a kiss.

And then tiny Owl and big Bernice were swept off round the hall by the rest of the Apaches as the heroines of the day.

The Fab Four celebrated that night with a midnight feast.

"Owly, what a star you are," said Eclaire.

"I couldn't have d-done it without you lot," said Owl, who had special permission from Ironglove to swap with Petula for the last night.

"What did *we* do?" said Flash and Lizzy.

"Oh, nothing," said Owl. "Nothing at all. Except m-make me come here. Make me do it. Make me dress up. Do drum rolls. Smile. Make me feel loved..."

There was a bit of a silence after this.

"Er," muttered Eclaire, breaking the silence, "all I can say is: here's to the FAB FOUR!"

"And didn't I help?" came a little voice.

"And what about *us*?!"

"Intruders!" squealed Flash.

Suddenly the cabin was filled with Brian, Bernice, Mathadi, Sylvie and Petula.

"Here's to the Naughty Nine," laughed Lizzy.

"What are you all doing? It's half past midnight!" came a stern adult voice.

Everyone dived under their bunks, which was a squash.

"What about *me*?" continued the voice. "Emily Smith! You wouldn't be here at all without me!"

Owl peered out from under Eclaire.

It was her mum, of course.

"Would you like to be an honorary member of the Terrible Ten, just for one night, Mrs Smith?" asked Eclaire in her politest voice.

"Why not?" smiled Owl's mum, before rounding up the intruders and herding them off to their beds.

But at 2am, four voices could still be heard chanting from a hut in Mohican Camp:

"All for one and one for all
Fatty, skinny, short and tall
Frizzy, Flash, Owl and Eclaire
Stick together, foul or fair.

"Four for one and one for four
Funny, clever, rich and poor
Frizzy, Flash, Eclaire and Owl
Stick together, fair or foul."

The Love Bug

Flash normally prefers mucking out to
making out, but when she meets the gorge
new stable lad, Tom, her favourite pony, Flame,
is quickly forgotten. Will Flash come to her senses
in time to save Flame from the knacker's yard?
And who's going to give Flash some top tips
on her make-up bag?

1-84121-476-0

Drama Queen

Owl's so shy she's never taken part in anything involving more than two people – even a conversation. But Owl's got big dreams and nothing's going to stop her being in the school play. Will she get the starring role or should she play something a little quieter, a piece of scenery perhaps?

More Orchard Red Apples

☐ **Bad Hair Day**	Ros Asquith	1 84121 480 9	**£3.99**
☐ **Frock Shock**	Ros Asquith	1 84121 482 5	**£3.99**
☐ **The Love Bug**	Ros Asquith	1 84121 478 7	**£3.99**
☐ **Drama Queen**	Ros Asquith	1 84121 476 0	**£3.99**
☐ **All for One**	Ros Asquith	1 84121 362 4	**£3.99**
☐ **Three's a Crowd**	Ros Asquith	1 84121 360 8	**£3.99**
☐ **Pink Knickers Aren't Cool**	Jean Ure	1 84121 835 9	**£3.99**
☐ **Girls Stick Together**	Jean Ure	1 84121 839 1	**£3.99**
☐ **Girls Are Groovy**	Jean Ure	1 84121 843 x	**£3.99**
☐ **Boys Are OK!**	Jean Ure	1 84121 847 2	**£3.99**
☐ **Do Not Read This Book**	Pat Moon	1 84121 435 3	**£4.99**

Orchard Red Apples are available from all good bookshops,
or can be ordered direct from the publisher:
Orchard Books, PO BOX 29, Douglas IM99 1BQ
Credit card orders please telephone 01624 836000 or fax 01624 837033
or visit our Internet site: www.wattspub.co.uk
or e-mail: bookshop@enterprise.net for details.

To order please quote title, author and ISBN
and your full name and address.
Cheques and postal orders should be made payable to 'Bookpost plc.'
Postage and packing is FREE within the UK
(overseas customers should add £1.00 per book).
Prices and availability are subject to change.